Neptune and the Litter Louts

Gerald Rose was Head of Illustration at Maidstone College of Art for many years, and is the author of *'AHHH!' Said Stork*, *Can Hippo Jump?* and *Penguins in a Stew/Give Us Your Coats*. He has also re-illustrated Charles Causley's classic collection of poems, *Figgie Hobbin*. Born in Hong Kong, Gerald now lives in Kent.

GW00809041

Neptune and the Litter Louts

Gerald Rose

A Young Piper Original
PAN MACMILLAN CHILDREN'S BOOKS

First published 1993 by Pan Macmillan Children's Books,
a division of Pan Macmillan Publishers Limited
Cavaye Place, London SW10 9PG

1 2 3 4 5 6 7 8 9

Text and illustrations © Gerald Rose

The right of Gerald Rose to be identified as author of this work
has been asserted by him in accordance with the Copyright, Designs
and Patents Act 1988

ISBN 0–330–32667–8

Printed in England by Clays Ltd, St Ives plc

This book is sold subject to the condition that it shall not, by way of trade
or otherwise, be lent, re-sold, hired out, or otherwise circulated without
the publisher's prior consent in any form of binding or cover other than
that in which it is published and without a similar condition including
this condition being imposed on the subsequent purchaser

Contents

The Ruined Garden

Neptune was King of the oceans and all the seas. He made sure the tides went in and out. He created storms and whirlpools.

"I can never rest," he complained. "The whales moan about the icebergs melting and the jellyfish grumble that the currents are too strong. What I need is a holiday. I shall go to my Summer Palace."

He harnessed the dolphins to his chariot and set off.

His Summer Palace was surrounded by a wonderful coral garden. Corals of every colour and shape grew there, graceful seaweeds waved gently, millions of sea-creatures swam, scrambled, hopped or crawled amongst the rocks and sandy clearings.

As Neptune entered his paradise it didn't seem like a paradise any more. A broken bottle, sinking down from above, almost knocked the crown off his head. There was a bad taste in the murky water. Horrible liquid oozed from a leaking metal drum. The dolphins choked and, for a moment, were blinded and crashed into the rocks.

"What is this?" Neptune gasped, as he stared in horror.

There were more broken bottles, rusty metal, plastic bags and tin cans littering his beautiful garden. Some of the coral was broken and smelly liquids gurgled and clung to the seaweed.

A loud sobbing made Neptune look up.
Through the murk he saw the sad shape
of Turtle as she struggled towards him.

"You've got to help me!" she sobbed.
"My eggs have been broken again! The
beach where I have always laid them,
where my mother laid her eggs, and
where my grandmother laid her eggs, has
been invaded."

By now Octopus, the Court Gardener,
had arrived.

"She's right," Octopus exclaimed. "While you have been away there have been some terrible changes. I've tried so hard to keep the garden clean but it's hopeless."

Neptune was sorry for Turtle and Octopus. "I will help you," he promised. "I'll find out who is causing all the trouble and make them clear it up."

Litter Louts

As soon as Neptune put his head out of the water a speed-boat roared by. Neptune covered his ears and then he held his nose – the stink of oil on the water made him feel quite ill.

A huge hotel had been built by the sea. The bay was crowded with all kinds of boats and there were hundreds of people sunbathing on the beach. A forest of parasols spiked the sand – no wonder Turtle's eggs were being broken.

Neptune tried to shelter behind some rocks but evil liquid poured out from a huge pipe and drove him away. All day he watched the visitors and saw that they just threw their litter away. At night there were barbecues on the beach and more litter.

A great shower of fireworks shot up from the deck of a large boat and cascaded into the sea. There was a noisy disco on board. As he drew closer he saw bottles and glasses thrown into the sea and rubbish just being tipped overboard.

Neptune Shows his Anger

Neptune was very upset but he decided to have a little fun with the boat party. First, he made the sea a little choppy. Lots of people began to feel quite sick. Then he made it very rough.

"We don't have enough life-jackets," the squabbling party complained.

Suddenly he stopped the waves and created a whirlpool so that the boat spun round and round.

"Someone has pulled out the plug from the bottom of the ocean!" cried the Captain. "*Help!*"

A great swordfish splintered the side of the boat.

"We are going to drown!" the cry went up.

Everyone tried to clamber into dinghies and life-rafts. Some people jumped into the sea and swam for the shore. The Captain danced about on the deck of his sinking boat.

"Save me!" he pleaded. "I can't swim!"
Suddenly the bow dipped right down into the sea and the stern rose up out of the waves. The Captain was left hanging on to the rail with water swirling round his knees. It was then that he noticed the tentacle . . .

Neptune's Palace

Slowly the tentacle wrapped itself round
his leg. The Captain had just enough time
to take a large gulp of air. He struggled
and wriggled but Octopus held him
firmly and carried him down, down, down
through curtains of frondy weeds. He was
left in a heap in a special room for visitors
in Neptune's palace.

When he opened his eyes he saw fish peering in at him through the window.

"Am I dreaming or did I drown?" he wondered.

Suddenly a voice behind him boomed,
"I am Neptune. You are my guest. Meet
Octopus. She saved you from drowning."
Octopus winked at the Captain.

"My name is Mr Bux," said the Captain importantly. He was not the kind of man to say "Thank you" to an octopus. "I want to get out of here," he demanded. "I own this island and the hotel. You can't do this to me. Take me home at once."

"You can go home when *you* have done something for *me*," replied Neptune. He took Mr Bux to the window. "That is your rubbish and you must clear it up."

"But – but – but —" began Mr Bux.

"*Silence!*" roared Neptune. "Either you clear it up or *else*!"

Mr Bux shook with fear. "I'll clear it up," he spluttered.

Octopus squashed Mr Bux into a special diving suit and set him to work.

Some Wet Work

A giant moray eel guarded Mr Bux and made sure that he did not try to escape. He had no intention of getting away. He was scared out of his wits.

The giant moray followed him everywhere. Whenever he stopped to rest it gave him a little nudge and showed its sharp teeth. Mr Bux had never worked so hard, scrambling over the craggy rocks in a bulky diving suit loaded down with rubbish.

At last he managed to build a huge pile
and hoped he had finished. But, as he
looked about him, he saw that more debris
was floating down and drifting into the
garden. When Neptune came out to see
how he was getting on Mr Bux was very,
very tired.

"I can never clean up your garden," he cried. "But if you let me go I will never drop rubbish again and I'll make other people stop too."

Neptune saw that Mr Bux was really sorry. "Do you promise?" he thundered.

"I promise. I promise!" cried Mr Bux. "I will do anything you say."

"If you don't you will be sorry," threatened Neptune.

Mr Bux was put into a large air bubble
and sent to the surface escorted by
Octopus who dropped him on a beach
where his friends would find him.

Who Believes in Neptune?

Mr Bux was just opening his eyes when his friends discovered him. He had swallowed a lot of water that tasted horrible. The bright sun blinded him and he had no idea how long he had been lying there.

"We thought you had drowned," cried his friends.

"What a storm!"

"That swordfish scared me stiff!"

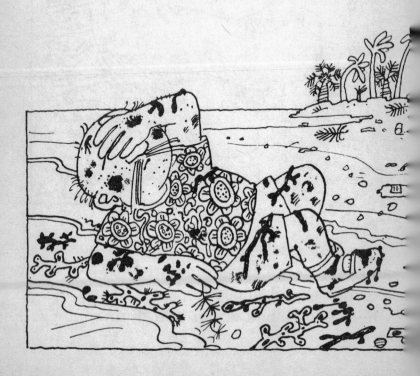

"What happened to you?" they asked.

Mr Bux told them about his adventure. He explained about the litter on the sea-bed and the smelly pipe running from the hotel, and he told them about Neptune and his wonderful garden.

His friends thought he was off his head.
"You're mad!"
"You've been lying in the sun too long."
"You've been dreaming."
They helped him back to the hotel.

He had a long soak in a warm bath, a few glasses of red wine, and a large plate of chicken and chips. He began to feel much better. Perhaps it was all a dream. Everyone else seemed to think so.

Mr Bux soon forgot his terrible fright and started building another hotel.

Intruders

Neptune really thought that Mr Bux would keep his promise but there was more mess than ever. Divers with spear-guns came nearer and nearer to the palace. They collected shells and coral from his garden. Boats dragged their anchors, breaking up the coral and damaging the palace.

Some of the sea-creatures started to fight back. They chewed the anchor ropes.

Crabs nipped noses.
Jellyfish stung toes.

Sea urchins pricked bums.

Neptune was very disappointed and angry that Mr Bux had not kept his word. There were more people, more smelly pipes, more noise and pollution in his sea. Turtle came back with her friends to ask Neptune if he had found a place where she could bury her eggs where they would be safe.

The Big Storm

Neptune was furious. "This time I will teach them a lesson they won't forget!" he shouted. "I will make a *super* storm."

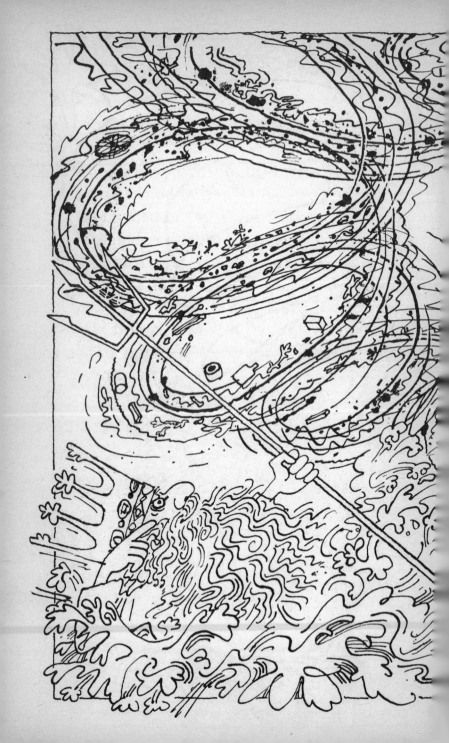

He summoned up all his powers and made the oceans heave and boil. The currents reached down to the bottom of the sea and picked up all the rubbish: the plastic containers, the plastic cups, rubber gloves, flip-flops, broken glass, globs of oil, rusty metal, soggy newspapers, broken bits of this and that . . . and tossed them all high in the air in a great spiralling, twirling, whirling waterspout.

Mr Bux watched the waterspout racing across the ocean. Then he remembered Neptune's warning. The waterspout came closer and closer until the roaring mass of rubbish hovered above the island.

What a Mess!

Down it came on to the visitors.

There was rubbish in their cars and rubbish in their beds.

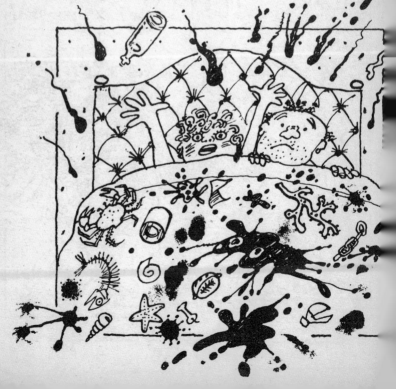

Yuk in their food and mud in their hair.

The muck and slime stuck to the windows of the hotel and to everybody's clothes. This was no place for a holiday. It was a nasty, dirty, stinky island now.

Everyone complained to Mr Bux.
"Clean out the swimming pool."
"Get this tar out of my hair."
"Just look at my BMW!"
"Buy me a new dress."
"There are green globs in my soup!"
"We want our money back."
He gave them their money back and
found that he had very little left. He was
ruined.

The Great Exodus

The visitors all wanted to leave at once.

"We will never come back to your rotten island."

"There is too much rubbish!"

"Too many nipping crabs."

"Too many jellyfish."

"Too many sea urchins."

But leaving the island was not easy. Their boats had been smashed to pieces or sunk in the great whirlwind. They would have to build new boats. Rubbish littered the whole island.

Some of it could be used.

They stuffed plastic bottles into sacks to make rafts.

They made boats from anything that floated.

Neptune's friends did all they could to help them on their way.

Soon the holiday-makers disappeared over the horizon.

When Mr Bux was quite alone Neptune paid him a visit.

"Oh, don't get angry," cried Mr Bux. "I won't cause any more mess."

"If you want to stay on this island you will have to make yourself useful," said Neptune.

Mr Bux worked very hard to show Neptune that he would keep his word. He dug great holes and buried the rubbish and to make sure that no one came back he put up notices all round the island.

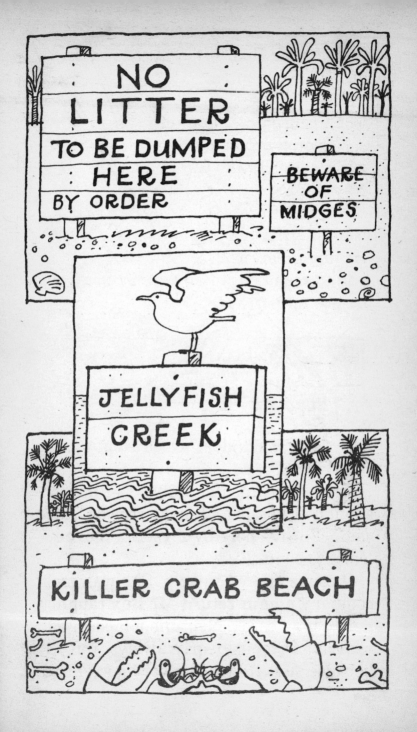

"What a good idea!" cried Neptune.
"Well done!"

Mr Bux grinned happily. "I've had
enough of hotels and noisy crowds," he
said. "I'll live here by myself. I'll even
learn to swim."

Octopus offered to help. She was great
company and in return Mr Bux taught
her to play cards. Neptune joined in as
well but Octopus nearly always won
because she often had a very good hand.

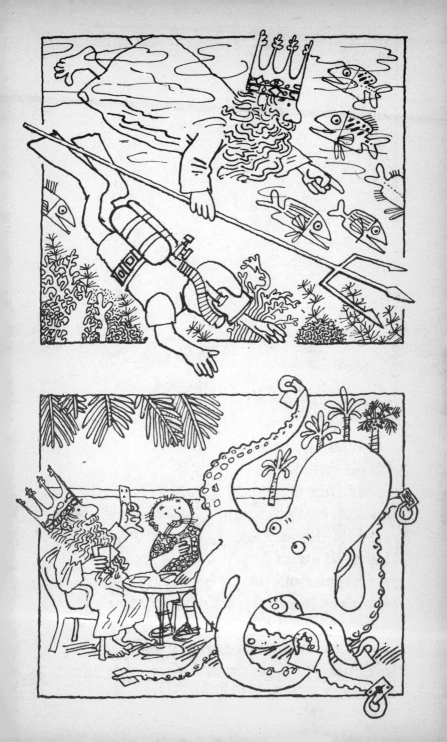

With whoops and squawks and chatterings the monkeys and birds moved into the hotels. The wind blew sand over the roads. Plants crept over the sand and grew up the stairs of the houses and hotels. They sneaked in through the windows and smothered the walls. Soon you would not have known that anyone had ever been there.

But it was Turtle and her friends who were happiest of all, because at last they were able to bury their eggs in the sand in peace and quiet.